*Title: **The Wild Side Fantasy***
*Subtitle: **Firefighter MF Romance Story***
*Author: **Ashlee Merrill***

From the Publisher:
Thank you for purchasing this book.

Table of Contents

Jane is not a plain lady. She was a student at the Art Institute of Chicago. She had fire engine red hair, but, as an art student, she referred to her hair color as "magenta." Jane enjoyed this endless assortment of 'normal' men. She loved to stand in contrast to them.

They were so different from the boys at her school. The boys at her school clung so desperately to their counterculture looks, their alternative tastes. They slouched at parties holding their drinks as if they'd practiced their facial expressions in the mirror for hours. Jane had gone to bed (or to the bathroom or to the lawn) with many of these boys and although many of these boys could talk the talk, they couldn't fuck the fuck. They were boring lays to her.

Much of this sex was some hurried version of the missionary position and there was some licking involved and that was about it. Jane fantasized about giving a wholesome, real, delicious man a chance to explore her wild side. And then she met with Rusty, an all-American man in his early thirties.

Chapter 1

Jane was not plain. She was a student at the Art Institute of Chicago. She had fire engine red hair, but, as an art student, she referred to her hair color as "magenta." She wore her hair in an old fashioned bob with bangs and people often mistook it for a wig. She had to touch up her dark brown roots every three weeks, as her hair grew rather quickly, by bleaching it first and then adding the "magenta" rinse. It was the purest of reds, she'd say.

She had her septum pierced, her nipples pierced, her navel pierced. Jane had a sprinkling of tattoos, in various places, both publicly visible and not. To the casual onlooker they appeared to all have been obtained on a whim, as there was no unifying theme, no single solitary work of art, but to Jane they were all purposeful and had profound meaning. She was short in stature and wore tight fitting clothes to show off her muscular physique. She lifted weights five times a week.

Jane worked at the flower shop two blocks down from the Art Institute. She enjoyed putting together flower bouquets on the spot for customers. They'd come in asking for something feminine, or something with jewel tones, or something that looked like wildflowers and she'd be able to put together an assortment within their price range. She enjoyed grouping the colors together, making sure there was a variety of forms, both rounded flowers and tall skinny flowers. She took pride in her little job.

She also took pride in being far more intelligent than she appeared. In school she wrote both essays and longer papers about things like the sexuality of Northern Renaissance still life painting, about the mixed political motivations behind criticisms of photographs by Andres

Serrano and Robert Mapplethorpe, about the movement of Russian Avant Garde to Stalinist Socialist Realism. However, her major was in ceramics. And although her professor considered her a savant at the potter's wheel, she preferred hand building, coil building human like sculptures. She had strong hands.

Jane's boss at the flower shop often called upon her to use her writing skills to write letters for the shop, letters to brides to let them know of their wedding estimates, retorts to nasty letters from angry customers who were upset about this detail or that.

At the flower shop there were regular customers and those who just dropped in once or twice. But there were other 'regulars' at the flower shop. There were the designers, who designed the flower arrangements, the drivers (the weekend drivers and the weekday drivers), the UPS man, the mail man, the flower shipment delivery man, the gift item delivery man (who delivered things like baskets, vases, gift cards and the like). Most of the customers to walk through the door of the flower shop were men.

Jane enjoyed this endless assortment of 'normal' men. She loved to stand in contrast to them. They were so different from the boys at school. The boys at school clung so desperately to their counterculture looks, their alternative tastes. They slouched at parties holding their drinks as if they'd practiced their facial expressions in the mirror for hours.

Jane had gone to bed with (or to the bathroom with, or to the lawn with) many of these boys and although many of these boys could talk the talk, they couldn't fuck the fuck. They were boring lays. Much of this sex was some hurried version of the missionary position and there was some licking involved and that was about it. But these men at the flower shop were wholesome, real, seemingly delicious. Jane fantasized about having a chance to sink her teeth into one of them, blow their minds with her wild side.

"Maybe the UPS man," Jane fantasized. Jane was confident. She liked that the UPS man's socks matched his uniform. She liked the way he said, "Sign here," with authority. She liked the way he hopped into his truck and drove off, as if into the sunset.

But this isn't the story of Jane and the UPS man. This is the story of how Jane met Rusty. Rusty was an all-American man in his early thirties. He was a firefighter and a new regular customer at the flower shop. Rusty was huge. Not only was he tall and very well built, but he sometimes came into the flower shop still in his firefighter gear, which seemed to make his feet larger, his legs longer, his shoulders broader. At first he came in once a week, on Fridays, getting flowers for his girlfriend.

He'd ask for something pink, or something orange, something simple, tulips, when he asked for lisianthus, a particularly delicate flower, Jane recommended special greens for him, when he asked for lavender roses Jane recommended a dried pink filler because baby's breath was too predictable, too obvious for that particular shade of rose. Jane took good care of Rusty. She was kind to him.

Rusty began coming to the shop on Wednesdays too. He began wooing his current girlfriend more aggressively. Rusty had a secret, a reason for this aggressive wooing. Rusty wasn't really your typical all-American boy next door all grown up.

Rusty was a sadomasochist. He had been that way as long as he could remember.

Whenever he saw comic books as a kid, and they showed damsels in distress and other boys were overwhelmed with the desire to rescue them, he was overwhelmed with how beautiful they looked right then and there. Every time he met a girl, every time he revealed his secret to her, she went running. Every girl. He was afraid his current girl would do the same.

He'd tried hiding his secret from girls, but that never lasted. A bite would always land on a nipple, a slap would always land on a cheek and the slap was often returned. He'd spent many a shameful and hurried evening purchasing pornography to relieve his tension. And although Rusty was a sadomasochist, he was still wholesome. He wasn't going to clubs and bars. He wanted to meet a "nice girl," not some bar slut.

His current girlfriend, Melissa, was a nice girl; she was a nurse's aid. He wanted to get it right with her. He wanted her to understand him, his desires, accept him. Thus, the wooing. But because Rusty had never gone to bars, had never tried online sex, had never become part of 'the community' Rusty had no clue as to how to verbalize his desires to another human being.

And he had no idea how to express himself sexually. He knew he liked the sight of a woman tied up, he knew he was overwhelmed with urges to bite and slap, he sometimes knew what he liked when he watched pornography, but all in all Rusty was a confused and conflicted man. He was at a complete loss because of his desire to remain "decent," and because of this desire he was doomed to fail with women again and again.

Jane picked up on the tension building in Rusty. Every time he came into the flower shop he was more and more nervous. Rusty felt as if he wasn't going to be able to hold back much longer. Something was bound to happen soon. One day, when he had picked out a dozen red roses filled with eucalyptus leaves Jane took in the sight of this massive, bulky, save-the-day type man wringing his hands. She felt bad for Rusty and wanted to ease his tension.

"You know if I didn't know any better I'd say you were about to pop the question or something. You're all nervous. You're buying more and more flowers. They're more and more expensive." Jane was blunt.

"Me? No. No. Not that. Just a big night. Hope she likes me," he stuttered.

Rusty was obviously a taken man and Jane was obviously not his type so it felt safe for Jane to speak her mind. "What do you have to worry about? You're totally hot, you're a firefighter, you're, like, a knight in shining armor. You'll be fine," said Jane, waving one hand in the air casually as she rung up his order.

"A knight in shining armor. That's funny," he responded and took his flowers and left. Jane didn't see him again for three weeks. and often wondered about her wholesome tortured knight.

Chapter 2

Jane woke up in her dormitory to the sound of a fire alarm. Again. It was likely to be another hippy burning too much incense. She stepped into her bunny slippers and wandered outside noting the time on her way out. It was 2:34. And it was cold. She had a morning class the next day. On her way out her shoulder bumped into Rusty's elbow as he was on his way in. They both turned around to look at each other.

Jane had seen Rusty in some of his gear before but not all of it. He looked massive. Jane looked tiny and compact. She was just over five feet tall and she had to put knots in her camisole straps to keep them from being too long and exposing her small breasts. As it was, they were still in danger of being exposed. The camisole was made of thin cotton and Rusty's eyes quizzically rested upon Jane's nipples.

"What? It's cold," Jane laughed nonchalantly, innocently. Guys have stared at her nipples like that before. She knew exactly why he was staring at her nipples. Rusty wasn't thinking about the hardness of Jane's nipples. He was thinking about the obvious piercings through them. Rusty was wondering why she had done that. Jane turned and walked away. She went to the fire truck and waited for Rusty there, her bunny slippered ankles crossed, her arms folded across her chest. Rusty finally came back out from the dormitory, mask under his arm.

"You can go back inside," he said.

"Are you at least gonna tell me who I can be pissed at?" Jane asked.

"You know I can't tell you that," Rusty replied.

"C'mon."

"I can tell you someone lit a candle and then put it inside a wooden bookshelf," said Rusty, rolling his eyes and smiling.

"Oh my God! The admissions committee selects us from far and wide. All over the world. We're supposed to be smart! This is ridiculous!" laughed Jane. It was pretty ridiculous.

Jane and Rusty shared a laugh at an anonymous student's expense. During their laugh Rusty stole glances of Jane, her tattoos, her pajama pants rolled down at the waistband revealing her abdominal muscles and part of a spider tattoo, those nipples, eyes laughing from behind smeared, slept-on eyeliner.

"I gotta go to bed. I have a morning class," said Jane turning around on her toes hesitantly and walking away, her firm, muscular buttocks protruding with each step.

"Jane!" What are you doing? She's in college. She's on campus. You're working! She did say you were hot... Jane turned back around, her finger in her mouth, her head down but eyes peering up with an over the top charm only an of-age college girl could pull off. "Do you want to get coffee sometime?"

Jane remarked, "That would be great. Yeah. I'll drop by the firehouse on my way to the flower shop Tuesday."

"Tuesday." Rusty smiled genuinely. Jane made him feel just plain good. She wasn't like the other girls, then again she wasn't what he was really looking for either.

Tuesday morning Jane got up at 10:30. She didn't have any classes on Tuesdays, she didn't have work on Tuesdays until 5pm. The flower shop was open until 8pm. Tuesdays were mostly free. Jane went to the gym, ran on the treadmill, lifted weights, came back to her dorm room and showered.

She washed and carefully set her hair. She opened her closet and contemplated what to wear. What does one wear? Out with a firefighter? Jane was excited to go out with a decent, normal guy. This was just what she had been fantasizing about. But why did he like her? Why had he invited her out?

She remembered the way he'd eyed her during their conversation, her tattoos, her piercings. She briefly considered "dressing down," dressing like more of a normal person, maybe a flower print dress, but then decided Rusty must like her for her. So she put on her usual skinny jeans, her favorite pair actually, with a white belt, converse, tight tee-shirt, and blue scarf knotted at her neck. She tossed her bag over her shoulder and walked to the firehouse.

When she got to the firehouse the garage door was open. She went through it and through the door at the opposite end of it and up a set of stairs. The stairs led to a kitchen where she found Rusty and two other firefighters cleaning up after an early lunch.

"Hi. Rusty," said Jane curtly, waving her hand in the air quickly, nervously. The sight of those other firefighters made her feel anxious, as if they had been caught in the raptures of their unacceptable love. But there was no love. Jane was just the girl on the other side of the counter for Rusty. And there was nothing unacceptable, Jane was twenty-one, of age to handle a relationship with a man in his early thirties. They just looked a little different.

"You must be Jane," said one of the firefighters, extending his hand. Jane shook it. "I'm Bob." Bob walked away.

"Hi. I'm Drew." Jane shook Drew's hand and Drew walked away.

"They sure left in a hurry," giggled Jane. "You been talkin' about me?"

"Maybe a little bit. Gotta warn the guys when a girl covered in tattoos is comin' to the firehouse."

"I know!" Jane said. "I don't wanna freak them out! So where do you wanna go? I see you have some coffee right there." She was hoping to stay at the firehouse, hoping things would move along quickly.

"Ah that stuff? That stuff is awful! You don't want that! I know a great place around the block."

"Skippy's? By the bookstore?" asked Jane. "I love that place!"

Rusty extended his arm to Jane, chivalrously and overly dramatically, having to bend his knees so she could reach him. He was well over six feet tall. Jane enthusiastically took his arm and they walked together to the coffee shop, closely, feeling each other's strides, feeling each other's sides pressed up against one another. They shared a silence with each other as they walked around the block to Skippy's.

Once seated, Jane had to ask, "So why are you a firefighter? What makes you want to run into burning buildings for a living? Why not be an accountant? That's safe."

"Well..."

Wow. Jane had gone to the heart of it right from the beginning. He could barely admit this to himself but he got off on seeing women tied up and tortured, so rescuing people seemed to make up for it, being a firefighter he really could be a knight in shining armor, at least momentarily, even though really he wanted things that seemed far more dark and evil. "My dad was a firefighter. So I thought I'd follow in his footsteps." Rusty grimaced.

Jane could see there was something else there and she knew she would get to the bottom of it.

Rusty could wait no longer. It was his turn to ask, "So why all the piercings. Why all the tattoos? Didn't all that stuff hurt?"

Jane exhaled. "I have a unique relationship with pain," she said, licking cappuccino foam off her thumb. Rusty raised an eyebrow. "Some things that are considered painful, I find enjoyable. Like my tattoos, some people like to go to their 'happy place' when they're getting tattooed, but not me. I like to really feel the pain. Really be there for it. And I consider all of these things adornments to my body. I take good care of my body, I work out, I'm just adorning it."

Rusty thought she had a nice body.

Rusty sipped his coffee. Jane enjoyed hers. They shared another silence having gotten out of the way what was bugging them each the most.

"So, you go to the Art Institute. That's supposed to be a good school. What kind of art do you do?" asked Rusty.

"I do ceramics. Hand building. Both figural and abstract," Jane answered, nodding. Rusty had no idea what she was talking about.

"I'd like to see it some time."

"You can come see it right now." Jane felt suddenly shy and withdrew. "If you have time."

"No. That'd be great. I'd love to see your... work," said Rusty. He was intrigued by this woman who had a 'unique relationship with pain.' He wanted more insight into her. This woman. This girl. She seemed to like him. He wondered what he was doing with her. But he paid for the coffee and offered her his arm again, she accepted it again, and they walked the three blocks to the Art Institute.

When they reached the ceramics studio no one was there. The door was locked and Jane rummaged in her bag for the key. Rusty stuffed his hands in his pockets and looked around. Jane opened the sticky door by ramming her shoulder into it. The studio was divided into three sections. On the right were several kilns and the left section was divided in the middle by floor to ceiling shelves filled with sculptures and bowls and cups. Behind the shelves were several potter's wheels, in front of them, several working tables.

"Well. This is my studio," Jane remarked, arms extended. "My sculptures are this way... Let me get the light." She reached for the light switches. Rusty reached for her hand on the light switch, ran his fingers along her arm, and paused at her shoulder. She looked up at him invitingly. God. Finally. She bit her own lip and turned down her perfectly lined eyes.

She wasn't a good girl, she wasn't what Rusty was looking for. Rusty had nothing to lose with Jane. He decided he'd give in to his desires. Just a little bit. He pushed her shoulder up against the wall with his hand. He grabbed the back of her head with the other and slouched down low enough that he could kiss her deeply, harshly, biting her lip, her tongue, his knees bent around her legs, his arms pressing her, enveloping her, the wall pressing on her back.

She was caged by his enormous body. Then he stopped, stepped back, wiped his mouth and waited for her response, half waiting to get slapped on the face again, half hoping to get kissed again.

"Not here," she said and she grabbed him by the wrist and led him to her dormitory. Menacing fantasies welled up in Rusty's mind during that walk. As did in Jane's. To her, here was her "normal" guy. She hadn't picked up on the biting, the pushing. To her, here was her chance to blow someone away with her freaky side. She unlocked her door and they both stepped in. Rusty looked around as he closed the door behind him.

Chapter 3

The ceiling was lined with a row of shelving filled with undulating pots and sculptures. There was a mirror with a dresser in front of it that had the remains of Jane's primping ritual atop it: rollers, scattered makeup, a fine toothed comb. Jane took a few steps backwards towards her bed. Rusty walked towards her. She pushed him. She was used to being the stronger one in the bedroom. All those skinny art school boys.

"So, do you have a roommate I should be worried about coming through the door?" asked Rusty. He was feeling confident now. He pushed her back. He was stronger than her.

"No. I'm a senior." Jane fell on the bed and laughed.

This laughter provoked Rusty. He was revealing himself to her faster than he had to any other woman and she was laughing at him? Or was she just having a good time? He pushed her down onto the bed and kissed her deeply, his legs kneeling around her legs, his arms bent around her shoulders. He used his right hand to undo her belt.

Crap. Jane had worn the tightest pair of jeans she owned precisely because they looked fantastic on her ass, NOT because they came off with ease in the bedroom. She had to do a special little dance just to get them on. Getting them off was a whole 'nother special little dance. Maybe she should've gone for the flower print dress. She hadn't expected things to happen so quickly with Rusty. Rusty was able to pull the belt from her pants with one swift gesture and Jane had renewed faith that, between the two of them, they could get her pants off with minimal clumsiness.

Rusty kneeled up over her. The way he looked at her, his eyes seemed chaotic, he seemed hungry. He pulled off each shoe without untying it and threw it across the room. He unbuttoned and unzipped her pants and pulled them off with two tugs, first to the knees, then clean off. She was impressed. She was wearing a blue g-string with orange trim. It seemed to match the scarf she was still wearing.

"Complimentary colors," she said, running her fingers along the trim and giggling. Rusty was so turned on by this incessant giggling and laughing because it provoked him, it inflamed him because it at once made him angry at the possibility she was laughing at him, and put him at ease that this whole thing was no big deal. Both emotions made him want to explore his more sinister side.

He savagely pulled up her shirt revealing her pierced nipples and navel and a number of tattoos but he left the shirt on, he left her scarf on and suddenly flipped her over. Jane felt shocked by his sheer strength, his strength over her. She wanted to rock some generic man's world but it was becoming clear it was her world that was about to be rocked.

She lay flat for just a moment and was lifted her by her belly with his arm into the kneeling position. He used both hands to slowly pull her g-string down, following the strings with his lips. Jane felt his tongue run down her ass, down her pussy. His tongue lingered there, savoring the taste of her, exploring her crevices irregularly, pausing here for a moment, pausing there for longer, licking the entirety of her slit several times to ensure he would taste the moisture that was building up inside of her.

He massaged her firm, unyielding ass as he did this, running his hands around each mound, squeezing it, pulling it open, pulling Jane open so he could see her, taste her. He left her panties around her knees. Jane felt a slight tinge of shame with them there. She wanted to keep them there. She wanted to curl up and take comfort in this bigger, older man's power over her.

All at once Rusty's lips and tongue and hands disappeared. Jane knelt below him, waiting to see what was next, immobile, blinking. Rusty knelt above her, looking down at her, her ass in the air, her shirt pulled up, a scarf around her neck. I have a unique relationship with pain. Rusty landed one single, solitary and very hard smack on Jane's rear end. Jane felt it on her skin, then in the muscles of her butt, then in her gut, then she felt it pulsate in her lungs. Then she felt a brief, "Ah-ah," come out of her mouth. She turned around to look at Rusty in surprise. Rusty's hand was still in the air, his mouth was open and he was looking at his hand. He looked at Jane.

"I'm sorry?" he said, an erection bulging through his tight jeans.

"Don't be. Do it again."

"I... I don't think so. I don't think I should," Rusty stammered, trying to ignore the erection that was now becoming quite evident through his jeans.

"Don't be silly," Jane laughed. "That was great." Jane arched her back, raising her ass higher in the air. She'd never been spanked before, but it was exhilarating. She was game to try anything new.

That laugh, Rusty shook it off. "No. Men aren't supposed to beat women." Rusty subconsciously stroked at his throbbing cock through his pants.

"You're not beating me, you're spanking me. There's a difference," she said, matter-of-factly. Jane slowly waved her ass from side to side, chin resting in her palms, waiting.

"Are you sure you want this?" Rusty asked.

"Sure. Look, if I get too freaked out or it hurts too much I'll just say alstromeria," Jane was now facing Rusty and was trying to comfort him. His erection was persistent despite the inner turmoil he was experiencing. Jane couldn't ignore it. She unzipped his pants and pulled it out. She cupped his testicles in one hand and stroked his cock with the other in a twisting motion.

Rusty exhaled and dropped back his head. Jane would lift her hand, twisting it with the skin of his cock and then twist it back on the way down, at the same time pulling at his balls. She leaned down and swallowed the head of his penis. It was enough to fill her entire mouth. She suckled on it, moving it in and out of her mouth, swirling her tongue around its head, all the while moving her hand up and down in this twisting motion, squeezing him with her strong ceramicist hands harder and harder, and pulling at his balls.

"Okay," Rusty sighed. Jane turned back around and arched her back even more this time and Rusty smacked her again and Jane felt the same sense of exhilaration, but this time, Rusty felt it too. For the first time in his life he felt it willingly. He smacked her again and again, harder and harder until Jane's ass was nearly purple and she belted out, "Oh my God!"

"Are you okay?" he asked, flipping her over so she was sitting down, facing him, knees up. Jane's body was languid, her lined eyes blinked lazily, she had drooled on the bed.

"I'm fine," said Jane, out of breath, a strand of magenta hair caught between her lips. She gave him two thumbs up and a smile and fell back onto her elbows. She put her feet on his chest and ran her right toes, nails painted green, down to his now completely engorged member. "How are you?"

Rusty took off his belt with the same single motion he used to remove Jane's and took off his pants. His legs were muscular. He kneeled at the foot of the bed and bit Jane's toes, he bit at her thighs, he bit her pussy, he bit the outline of her abdominal muscles, he bit her nipples, he bit her lips, he showered her in caresses of painful kisses to which Jane occasionally responded with an, "Ah."

Once he reached her lips Jane bit him back. He bit her harder, tugging at her lower lip as though he were going to pull it off and grabbed her scarf at the knot stopping to make sure this was okay. Jane nodded. He pulled the knot down to the mattress choking Jane and he pressed himself into her. Jane let out a gurgled moan.

He thrust himself into her slowly at first, like he always had with women, breathing into her ear. But the sound of her altered, obstructed breath provoked him like nothing ever had. He stood up on his hands and began pumping himself into her as hard as he could, rhythmically, in a somewhat rounded motion, his right hand still pressing down at the knot of Jane's scarf.

He pushed himself into her so hard that the whole lower half of her body was raised up to Rusty, who was kneeling on the bed. Jane was hypnotized by this rhythm, this fucking, she touched her body, she pulled at her nipples, her clit, trying to recreate the special kisses he had bestowed upon her.

She tried to kiss Rusty but Rusty just pushed her down by her forehead. His cock was long and thick, the head of which was even thicker and with every motion Jane could feel its contour in her. He pushed her inner labia in and out, her juices mixed with his until finally there was nothing but a suction sound and the occasional sound of the two mouths exhaling.

Rusty rolled her over on top of him and held her body up over him by her neck. He pressed her legs open with his and thrust into her with cadence and momentum. This position seemed to particularly excite Jane as Rusty rubbed his body against her clit with every forceful push. She let out a hindered exhalation or moan or whimper with each drive into her body.

Rusty, still holding her by the neck threw her onto the floor. He jumped onto her. He kneeled above her and looked at her like an animal might look at prey. His cock was wet from her juices now and he placed her feet onto his chest. He placed his fingers onto her anus. She looked at him and relaxed. He slowly slid his soaking wet cock into her ass, millimeters at a time, watching her face, taking care not to hurt her. But once he was in all the way he began moving in and out, faster and faster.

She was so tight, she was such a tiny girl. Jane braced herself with one hand on the bottom of the dresser and one hand on the bottom of her desk. She felt carpet burn forming on her lower back, a point of pride.

He was so big, her mouth was open out of sheer shock that she, such a petite woman, was even able to take in such a huge man. Rusty began driving himself into her harder and harder, more and more rhythmically until finally Rusty couldn't manage the rhythm anymore, he pulled out and came all over Jane's perfectly formed abdominals.

"Oh my God. I'm sorry. Are you okay? I'm so sorry. Are you okay?" Rusty was flustered, and ashamed.

"It's cool! I'm all right. Here. Let me get a towel for you... us." Jane giggled, out of breath, flustered too. She got a towel and they silently wiped off the evidence of Rusty's deepest, darkest secret. Jane pushed Rusty gently back into the bed and curled up into his big arms. He had shown her something new in so many ways, he wasn't like the art school boys in so many ways. He was just a regular guy on the outside, but in the bedroom he was a wild animal, he had shown her a side of herself she couldn't believe she hadn't explored before.

She was grateful to Rusty as she lay there, running her fingers through the chest hairs that stuck out from his tee-shirt. They both lay there in their tee-shirts, but Rusty's mind was in a different place. He felt shame in what he had done to Jane. He felt it was wrong, wrong to treat a woman, a girl like that. He felt shame in what he had done, but at the same time Jane felt so good in his arms, so tiny, she made him feel big, masculine.

Jane popped her head up. "What time is it?"

"Four twenty," Rusty said, looking at his watch.

"I gotta get ready for work!" Jane said, hopping out of bed, kissing Rusty on the lips, pausing to smile at him. Rusty looked away. "Hey," she said, grabbing his face in her hands, "This was fantastic. I mean it." Jane got out of bed and walked over to the dresser; she picked up the fine toothed comb and carefully ran it through her disheveled hair, finishing it off with her hand.

"Do you think we could have coffee again?" Jane asked lightheartedly as she did her tight skinny jeans dance.

"Yeah, sure. Drop by the firehouse," said Rusty, laughing a little at Jane's jeans dance, feeling a little optimistic because he was still feeling the warmth of Jane's body in his arms. She felt so right there. He put on his pants and his belt and discretely left the building.

Jane dropped by the firehouse the very next day. She wanted to know more about her wholesome tortured knight. Where did he go to school? Who did he go to the prom with? Did he always want to be a firefighter? What was his favorite color? What was his favorite food? When she walked up the stairs and into the kitchen Rusty was sitting at the table eating a bowl of chili and Bob was washing dishes.

"Hi Rusty. Hi Bob," Jane said.

"Heyyy, Jane! Didn't think we'd see ya back so soon! How are ya?" asked Bob shaking Jane's hand overly enthusiastically.

"I'm good. Thanks! How are you?"

"Good," said Bob, exhaling and rubbing his slight belly. "Your friend here is an excellent chef. You should try some of his chili."

"Really?" said Jane inquisitively. "I had no idea." She faked a pouty glare at Rusty who continued to look down into his bowl. Bob noted the tension and excused himself. Jane spun around and plopped herself in Rusty's lap, wrapping her arms around his neck and crossing her legs. Rusty stiffened but he couldn't ignore her there. She ran her finger along his profile, down his forehead, his nose, and along his lips. This seemed to weaken this stubbornly distant man momentarily.

"Rusty? What's the matter?" She pouted some more.

"I just..." Rusty searched for the courage. "I just don't think what we did was right. I don't think what was between us was right."

"But Rusty, don't be silly," Jane ran her fingers through his hair and looked carefully at each feature on his face, his well defined lips, his full eyebrows, she looked back and forth between each speckled blue eye. "What we shared was wonderful. For you and for me. We can be ourselves around each other. It doesn't matter how different we look."

"No. A man shouldn't do that to a woman. I'm sorry Jane. You bring out bad things in me, things I need to overcome." Rusty scooted his chair out and stood up and, in doing so, pushed Jane off his lap. Jane stumbled. He went to the sink and washed his bowl, turning his back to Jane. "I think you should go."

"Rusty are you sure? Have you thought about this? Don't you remember –"

"Go!" Rusty cut her off. He didn't want anyone hearing any of the details of their encounter. He felt nothing but shame, he remembered nothing but wickedness. He'd already forgotten the sense of freedom he felt the second time he spanked her and allowed himself to enjoy it, he'd already forgotten the sense of power he felt when he was choking her and fucking her harder than he'd fucked anyone before, he'd forgotten how masculine he felt holding her tiny body in his arms.

Jane scoffed. She dropped her hands to her thighs. She turned around and walked out of the firehouse. For the next six months Jane and Rusty searched for each other in other people. Rusty searched for Jane in "good girls." He sought out diminutive women, women who laughed a lot, women who loved art. But his relationships always failed; Rusty never could gain control over his passions and these good girls always left him.

Jane searched for Rusty in her circle of art school friends. She looked for well built muscular boys, she desperately searched for someone to spank her, to bite her, she positioned boys' arms to mimic the way she walked arm in arm with Rusty, but none of it felt right. No one fit the bill. It never worked when she had to tell them to spank her, tell them to grab her by the arm. Rusty never returned to the flower shop. Neither of them ever returned to Skippy's.

Whenever Jane walked past the firehouse on the way to the flower shop she quickened her pace, for fear of running into Rusty, seeing him washing the fire truck or sliding down the pole on the way to a call. Whenever Jane walked past the firehouse on the way to the flower shop the scab of that moment in the kitchen was torn off and she felt the pain of being thrown out all over again. Jane started going the long way, around the block to avoid the firehouse altogether. She wished things had gone differently, but as it was, she never wanted to see Rusty again.

Chapter 4

Jane was on a date with Thomas. She had been on lots of dates with lots of guys since Rusty but Thomas seemed different. He had read all the right books. He liked all the right art. He said all the right things about Jane's sculptures. He wasn't a sadomasochist per se, but was at least willing to try things in the bedroom under Jane's guidance. He wore black rimmed glasses and messy blond hair.

He was the same age as Jane. He was skinny, but Jane was willing to forgive this flaw. It was Wednesday night and he and Jane were hanging out in her bedroom after a poetry reading on campus.

"I thought she was amazing!" said Jane.

"She was alright," Thomas put in. "I don't know. Maybe I'm just not into Black Lesbian Poetry. Maybe I just can't relate."

"I'm not black. I'm not a lesbian. I can relate. I can appreciate it," Jane capitulated.

Thomas took off Jane's jacket and placed it on her chair. Then he took off her tee-shirt. She was wearing a turquoise bra and removed. He let her do her skinny jeans dance herself. He did his own skinny jeans dance out of his black skinny jeans.

They performed this ritual almost robotically, as though they had performed it a thousand times. They climbed onto the bed, Jane first, crawling, Thomas sighing because he knew what this crawling meant.

Jane stopped mid-crawl and looked back at Thomas. Thomas knew what to do. He slapped her ass. Jane felt a slight sense of relief from her tension. She was glad to have had found someone who was willing to humor her, willing to be somewhat adventurous in the bedroom. Maybe, she'd hoped, maybe he'd get a paddle. Thomas was willing to spank and bite, but that was it. Jane was beginning to believe that was enough for her. Jane was becoming genuinely happy with Thomas. He wasn't tortured. He never kicked her out. And he was more like her. He had tattoos. He dressed like her.

But their pseudo role play was interrupted. There was a knock at the door.

"Just a minute!"

Jane quickly threw on a tee-shirt that had probably been lying on the floor for a week and answered it.

Rusty was on an early weekday date with Carol, a fifth grade school teacher. She had shoulder length blond hair that fell in locks upon her shoulders. She was wearing a red and pink floral printed dress with short sleeves and a red, shiny belt. It was their fifth date. Rusty walked her home around seven thirty and she invited him in.

"Do you want a cup of coffee?" asked Carol from her kitchen as Rusty paced nervously in her living room.

"No. I'll take another beer if you have one."

"Aren't you sure you've had enough?" Carol warned.

"I weigh 274 pounds, I'm six foot four. Carol, I can handle a few beers," said Rusty, condescendingly. The truth was, Rusty was a little drunk already. He was nervous. He knew it was about that time, as it was with all his relationships, that his true nature would be revealed and Carol's commitment to him would be tested. Carol was so nice, so pretty.

"Well okay," said Carol, popping open another beer for Rusty and handing it to him. They stood across from one another, looking into each other's eyes in the hallway in between Carol's kitchen and her living room/dining room space. Rusty chugged his beer.

"If I didn't know any better, I'd think you had something to be nervous about," said Carol, tapping him on the chest and walking over to the couch, hesitating before she sat down. "Do you have something to be nervous about?"

Rusty came over to the couch and sat down. He ran his fingers through her hair and grabbed the back of her neck. He kissed her deeply, trying to express his powerful emotions to her. He pressed her head into his with one hand, massaging her shoulder forcefully with the other. Carol pulled away from his advances.

"You're so forward tonight," she said.

"I guess I'm just really feeling strongly. You look so incredibly beautiful."

Carol blushed. She was dressed in a very old fashioned dress, one that one of those damsels in distress might have worn. She would have looked stunning tied to a pair of railroad tracks, her red lips contorted into a scowl, her hands fully extended trying to break free from the rope, her red pumped feet kicking in vain.

Rusty was getting sidetracked but he couldn't get that image of Carol out of his head. Those pumps, that dress with the thin red belt, those lips. He had to possess her like that. He grabbed her by the shoulders and kissed her once on the lips, decisively. She laughed. Rusty immediately remembered the way Jane had laughed, the way her laugher at once incited him and indicated to him everything was okay, that he was okay.

Rusty took this laugh as the go-ahead. He pushed Carol down onto the couch and lay on top of her. He smothered her with his weight. He ran his fingers through her hair again, this time pulling it a little. He pressed on her shoulders with his hand. He squeezed her breast hard, pulling at her nipple.

"Stop Rusty. You're hurting me! What are you doing?" Carol exclaimed. "This isn't the gentle Rusty I know." She pushed him off of her.

"Yeah well..." Here it was again. The end of another relationship. Rusty slurred his speech. "The gentle Rusty you know isn't so gentle deep down."

He was drunk. Now he'd said something that surprised even him. He had admitted to himself, out loud, and to Carol, that he was not a gentle man when it came to women. And in his thirty-three years in existence there was only one other person, including himself, who not only didn't find this appalling, but found it interesting and desirable. Jane. He had to find her.

"Get out," said Carol with certainty. Rusty looked at his watch. It was 7:50. He just might make it to the flower shop. "What? Do you have some place you need to be you... you jerk?"

"Yeah, actually I do," said Rusty, and he ran out of the apartment and ran straight to the flower shop. He arrived just as the owner was locking the door. Rusty had to beg him to let him in.

"It's for Jane. Please." Rusty clasped his hands together.

The owner sighed as he dropped his tired head and let Rusty in. "Only a cut flower bouquet," he said, pointing his finger in the air, as they walked back towards the flowers. "I'm not doing any arrangements. I'm done designing for the day."

"Jane isn't here?" asked Rusty.

"Nope. You're stuck with me." The flower shop owner was a 38 year old gay man who resembled a very lean, well formed gorilla in build, body hair, and facial features. He worked out frequently and was very proud of his 32 inch waist. His forearms were particularly muscular and hung down low next to his slender thighs, hands curled up almost into fists.

"Well. What kind of flowers does she like?" asked Rusty, flustered, hurried, and obviously desperate. And drunk. The flower shop owner took pity on him, sighed again, and dropped his head down to the side. What a crime it was that such a strapping young man was to be straight.

"She likes masculine flowers."

"What does that mean?" asked Rusty.

"It means Cymbidium orchids and tall grasses, but you..." the flower shop owner pointed at Rusty up and down indicating the train wreckage, "...You are going to need roses too." So the flower shop owner put together a bouquet of various kinds of orchids, tall leaning grasses and he began to cut some of the roses short, at different heights.

"Wait! Shouldn't the roses be long?" Rusty asked.

"Trust me. Your girl knows flowers. She knows they'll look better at varying heights and that they'll last longer the shorter they're cut. I know what I'm doing. Let me do my job here."

"Sorry."

"And," the owner added, "She's got this new thing now. She likes the thorns to be left on the roses. I don't know what that's all about. Should I leave them on or shave them off?" he asked, knife in hand.

Rusty smiled. "Leave them on, please."

The owner finished off the bouquet, wrapped it in tissue paper and clear cellophane and tied it off with matching ribbons of which he curled the edges.

"That'll be 75 dollars."

Rusty whistled and paid up. He walked straight to Jane's dormitory. The outside door was locked. It was cold outside. It was a weeknight and it was 8:30 now. No one was going in or out of the building. Finally, after about twenty minutes a group of three kids that all looked like they could be Jane's friends walked into the building. Rusty stood up from the stoop and asked them if they'd let him in. They refused; they didn't like the looks of him and they left him out there, flowers in hand.

Then, a pair of girls came out of the building about forty minutes later and Rusty was able to catch the door and get into the building. Rusty remembered the room and stood in front of it for a good minute, his right hand in the knocking position, his left hand holding a very expensive flower bouquet which he didn't think was very pretty. Finally he knocked.

"Just a minute!" It was Jane. There was some rustling and Jane cracked the door open just a little bit but just enough to see Rusty.

"Rusty!"

Jane stepped out of her room and closed the door behind her. She was wearing an oversized Ramones tee-shirt and nothing else. "What are you doing here?" she whispered, eyeing the flowers.

"I don't know. I mean. I'm here to see you. I missed you Jane. I was wrong. I'm so sorry." Rusty offered her the flowers. He was so sappy. Jane was taken by this. None of the guys in her circle of her friends bothered with flowers, with anything like this.

"Um. I'm sort of not alone," said Jane.

"I see," said Rusty, giving Jane the flowers. "I'll leave you be."

"No. Wait. Um. Don't go. You weren't alone tonight either." Rusty looked at Jane quizzically. "Lipstick on your mouth," Jane said, pointing to her own lips. Rusty wiped it off. "Just give me a second to break it off. Wait here." Jane went inside with the flowers, admiring them on the way in.

Rusty leaned against the wall of the dormitory, his head swimming in beer and thoughts of Jane. About fifteen minutes later a slender boy came out of Jane's room. He wore tight black jeans, black rimmed glasses, and messy hair. He looked Rusty over and smirked. Rusty was surprised by his audacity. He could have snapped the boy in half.

Jane invited Rusty in. She was dressed now.

"Thank you for the flowers. You left the thorns on." Jane smiled and turned her eyes down. "Working at a flower shop, no one ever thinks to buy you flowers." Jane hesitated. "Is this really a change of heart? You're drunk."

"Jane. I want to learn more about myself with you. I want to hold you in my arms. I want to tie you to trees. I want to take you to my mother's picnic next weekend." Rusty was being very enthusiastic.

"That's nice to hear," Jane replied, excited about the holding and tying part, not so much so about the picnic part. "But are you sure about that picnic? I'd stick out like a sore thumb."

"I don't care. I don't care because with you I can be myself. I keep going out with these other women, trying to be someone I'm not and it just doesn't work. I keep hoping that one day one of them will accept me for me, when someone already has. You. You accepted me even before I accepted myself."

"It's true," said Jane, walking over to Rusty, "I do like your freaky side." He was sitting at her desk chair facing outwards into the bedroom. She sat in his lap and wrapped her arms around his neck. "How do I know you aren't going to push me away tomorrow or the next day?"

"There's nothing I can do to prove it to you at this very moment except to not do it to you tomorrow, or the next day, or the next. Jane, I want to be with you. I want to let go of all these lies I've been telling myself all my life. I want to feel for the rest of my life the way I felt when I was with you. Powerful. Masculine." Free. Accepted.

Rusty was remarkably insightful for a drunken man. Jane knew it was not only difficult for Rusty to share these things with another human being, but difficult to admit to himself. She kissed him sweetly with her eyes closed.

She opened her eyes to see his reaction. He was still leaning forward from the kiss, his eyes starting to open. She tilted her head back and parted her lips, offering herself up to him. He grabbed her head with both hands and kissed her powerfully, deeply, massaging her scalp, messing her bright hair, running his hands around her neck and back behind her head to press it harder into his.

He stood up, grabbing Jane by her thighs and wrapping them around his waist, her arms still around his neck, and he walked over to the bed and crawled on to it. For a moment, Rusty knelt on the bed and Jane hung from him by her legs and arms, attached at the lips. He rested her on the futon mattress and began pressing her.

He pushed her arms up over her head and pressed them down into the bed at the elbows, then at the wrists, as if deciding which restraint he preferred. He had so much to learn. He pressed on her shoulders, her breasts. He pressed her legs open and down towards the bed. They didn't want to bend because Jane's jeans were so tight so he pulled the jeans down to her knees.

He felt around for her panties but found nothing. He stopped. He looked around Jane's legs to her face. She gave him a naughty smile. She wasn't wearing any panties. Rusty knew she knew he was coming in and she didn't put any on. He savagely pulled her pants off the rest of the way. She jumped onto her knees and pulled off her tee-shirt. She was naked and adorned. Rusty took off his clothes.

"I got something I think you'll like. I dunno," said Jane shrugging.

"What is it?"

"You'll see," replied Jane, innocently.

Jane was still kneeling down on the bed as she rummaged under it, left hand supporting her on the floor, right hand looking for this mysterious item. Her ass was high up in the air and Rusty could contain himself no longer.

He slapped her on the left butt cheek. Jane stopped rummaging. She put her right hand down on the ground cautiously. She raised her ass up into the air and Rusty slapped her again. Jane looked back at him; he looked at her. She nodded. He slapped her ass over and over again, Jane letting out an, "Oh my God," or an, "Ah."

When Rusty's hand hurt he stopped. He massaged Jane's ass and she returned to rummaging under the bed. As she did this Rusty stuck his fingers into her pussy, into her ass, moving them in and out, feeling the thin wall in between, feeling the wetness he had caused inside of her, feeling the skin of the openings. Finally, Jane popped up from under the bed and Rusty pulled his fingers out of her, she was smiling and a bit out of breath, holding up a pair of handcuffs.

"I thought you might like these," she said, dangling the cuffs from her forefinger. She was proud of her find yet somewhat unsure of what his response to it might be. "What do you think?"

Rusty tore into her like an animal. He grabbed the cuffs from her and pushed her onto her back. He strapped the cuffs around her neck, so that one wrist of the cuff was on one side of her neck and the other wrist was on the other side. He was pressing them into the bed, choking Jane. He tore into her mouth with his.

He kept the cuffs around her neck and nibbled at her pierced nipples, flicking his tongue at them intermittently. He kneeled up and peeled the cuffs from Jane's neck, the impression of their links still pressed into her flesh. He held them up and wondered what to do with them, what extremities shall he lock for his very own? What a wonderful gift this woman had waiting for him. He was so glad he came.

All at once Rusty knew what to do. He took Jane's left ankle and cuffed it to a slat high up on Jane's futon bed so that Jane's leg was spread open. Jane giggled and laughed at this. He was so relieved to hear this laughter. He grabbed her other leg and placed it on his chest. He lifted her pelvis up to meet his and he fucked her hard.

He fucked her so hard her breasts looked like they were going to shake off her chest. He fucked her so hard Jane had to brace herself to keep from banging her head on the bed and was only just barely successful. He fucked her so hard they both began sweating profusely and all you could hear was the pounding and slapping of muscular flesh and the occasional single minded grunt.

Rusty occasionally leaned down to bite Jane. He would fill his mouth with her side or her breast or her ear. Twice he slapped her across the face and both times she responded with open mouthed laughter which only caused Rusty to fuck her even harder. Jane began fucking Rusty back, she began grinding into him as he thrust himself into her. She became more vocal.

She began to writhe, to pull at her hair, bite her own fingers, lips. Sensing she was about to cum Rusty bit at her nipples and placed one hand over her neck to brace himself and continued fucking her in that exact same pace. She threw a complete fit, pushing his hand away, sitting up in the bed, screaming, grabbing him close with her leg, shaking her head, fucking him sitting up. Rusty could feel her insides trembling, seizing, he came too. He couldn't help it.

Rusty gently uncuffed Jane's ankle from the bed. He kissed it and laid down beside her.

"Maybe next time we could get some candles and you could pour the wax on my nipples," Jane said lightheartedly.

"Would that be nice for you?" Rusty asked, never having heard of that before.

"It sounds amazing," Jane said. "And romantic... maybe we should invest in some rope."

"Whoa. Let's not get ahead of ourselves here."

"What? You're the one asking me to your mom's picnic. I've just been doing a little bit of reading. I'm curious."

"Okay. Rope it is." Rusty hesitated. "Do you think you could wear one of those flower print dresses, that go just beneath the knee?"

"Oh my God. I have the perfect thing," said Jane, hands in the air as if to say, 'Hold on.' And she went to the closet and pulled out a vintage 1940's flower print dress. It was pink and green and had a shiny green buckle on the side of the waist. It matched her toenail polish. She pressed the dress on its hanger up against her waist and modeled it for Rusty. It was just like in the comic books. "I love vintage," she said, like the excited school girl she was.

"It's perfect," Rusty said and smiled. "Do you think you could put it on?" Jane tossed the dress over her head, zipped it most of the way, and asked Rusty to zip it the rest of the way.

"Wait," she said. And she rummaged in her closet momentarily and came out with a pair of natural leather heels. She slipped them on, combed her hair, lined her lips, and put on pink lipstick. She stretched out her arms.

"How do I look?" she asked, smiling.

"I wish we had some of that rope right now," said Rusty, walking up to her, still naked, and bending his knees so he could run his hands along the dress, along Jane's ass, her back, her breasts. He messed her hair again. He grabbed her by the head with his forefingers behind it and his thumb at her mouth and he smeared her lipstick across her face. Jane melted into his hand. Still holding onto her head he leaned down and back and grabbed the handcuffs off the bed and cuffed Jane's wrists behind her back. He pushed down on her shoulders. She knelt in front of him, facing him. He was hard again, the sight of her in that dress, the thought of her tied up in rope, willingly for him.

Jane opened her mouth and licked the tip of his cock, she licked around the ridge of its head, but she had no resistance. Her hands were cuffed behind her back. So Rusty grabbed her by the sides of her head and pushed her onto him, and off of him, and onto him again.

He pushed himself into her so deeply she gagged but when he looked down at her she continued to push her head forward. She wanted this. And with each gag more saliva came up from her throat, with each push of her head his cock became wetter and wetter until he had to pull her head off of him to keep from cumming. A trail of wetness led from her mouth to his cock as she knelt there looking up at him expectantly, proud of herself, of what she'd done to him. Rusty felt overwhelmed.

He turned her around on the carpet, burning her knees as he did so. Jane took in a "Hiss," as she inhaled. He pushed her face sideways down into the carpet so that he was pressing on her right cheek, her hands were behind her back, and her ass was in the air. He lifted her dress up to her waist.

He spit on her ass and Jane relaxed. Rusty pressed the head of his literally dripping wet cock into her ass slowly until her anus closed around it. He slid into her, his left hand still pressing on her right cheek, his right hand grabbing her thigh, pressing her onto him. He began thrusting himself into her with force, pausing in between each thrust, pushing Jane's face harder into the carpet each time.

This pace, this pose, these cuffs, this position of the dress was all very exiting to Jane and she spread her knees open along the carpet, feeling each fiber on her sore knees along the way. She could feel Rusty's balls swinging around to her clit with each thrust and with each thrust she was more aroused, more relaxed. Rusty let out a moan and suddenly began to quicken his pace, he let go of Jane's face and grabbed her with both hands by the thighs. He pounded at her ass until his pace became irregular and he thrust himself deeply into her, holding her, throbbing inside of her.

Rusty uncuffed Jane for the second time that evening, but he wasn't done with her. Out of breath, he gestured for her to touch herself. Jane felt the remains of Rusty in her pussy and now in her ass. She licked her fingers and looked up at him.

She touched her cheek; it was abraded. She touched her knees; they were abraded. She pulled hard at her nipples through the dress and hissed. Jane sat back and bent her knees up. She pulled up her dress. She stuck a finger from her left hand in her pussy, moving it in and out slowly, as if beckoning Rusty's fluids to come out. Then she stuck another finger in her pussy and began moving in and out with more rhythm.

She licked her forefinger from her right hand and began massaging her clit. This hand moved hurriedly from her clit to her nipples and back. Rusty noticed this and took over squeezing her nipples for her. He'd squeeze them hard, then pull them out, then shake them. He unbuttoned the front of her dress so he could lick her nipples and then blow on them, freezing them.

He kissed and bit her lips, her ears. Jane felt her cheek and her knees, she looked Rusty in the eyes and began moving her finger in and out of herself with greater vigor, touching her clit with more abrasion until finally her heaving and sighing became so loud Rusty covered her mouth. Her convulsing body became stiff and then limp. Rusty lifted her to the bed, laid her down, and sat next to her, running his fingers through her hair.

"I have NEVER done that in front of anyone before," said Jane.

"I've never done a lot of things before," said Rusty. "You look beautiful."

Rusty and Jane stood in front of his mother's door a week and a half later having rung the doorbell. Rusty held his chili. Jane held her cornbread.

"I didn't know you baked. I didn't even know there was an oven in your dorm. How did you even know I was making chili?"

"I have my ways. Besides, I figured chili was the only thing you could make," said Jane. She smiled at Rusty and looked at the door, waiting for it to open. Rusty eyed her as a soft breeze gently lifted the hem of her flower print dress.

THE END

www.ingramcontent.com/pod-product-compliance
Lightning Source LLC
Chambersburg PA
CBHW030417160726
47992CB00007B/3164